SO-AYO-803

CONELY BRANCH LIBRARY
4800 MARTIN
DETROIT, MI 48210
(313) 224-6461

SEP

JUL '06

MAR '16

NOV -- 2002

Tools

Search

Notes

Discuss

▶ MyReportLinks.com Books

Go!

PRESIDENTS

HERBERT HOOVER

A MyReportLinks.com Book

David A. Y. O. Chang

MyReportLinks.com Books

an imdrint of

Enslow Publishers, Inc.

Box 398, 40 Industrial Road
Berkeley Heights, NJ 07922
USA

CONELY BRANCH

MyReportLinks.com Books, an imprint of Enslow Publishers, Inc.

Copyright © 2002 by Enslow Publishers, Inc.

All rights reserved.

No part of this book may be reproduced by any means
without the written permission of the publisher.

Library of Congress Cataloging-in-Publication Data

Chang, David A.
    Herbert Hoover: A MyReportLinks.com Book / David A.Y.O. Chang.
        p. cm. — (Presidents)
    Includes bibliographical references and index.
    Summary: A biography of the thirty-first president of the United States, describing his
career as mining engineer, businessman, and president during the Great Depression.
Includes Internet links to Web sites, source documents, and photographs related to
Herbert Hoover.
    ISBN 0-7660-5006-8
    1. Hoover, Herbert, 1874–1964—Juvenile literature. 2. Presidents—United
States—Biography—Juvenile literature. [1. Hoover, Herbert, 1874–1964. 2. Presidents.]
I. Title. II. Series.

E802 .C47 2002
973.91'6'092—dc21
[B]
                                                                                    2001004304

Printed in the United States of America

10 9 8 7 6 5 4 3 2 1

To Our Readers: We have done our best to make sure all Internet addresses in this book
were active and appropriate when we went to press. However, the author and the Publisher
have no control over, and assume no liability for, the material available on those Internet
sites or on other Web sites they may link to. The Publisher will try to keep the Report Links
that back up this book up to date on our Web site for three years from the book's
first publication date. Any comments or suggestions can be sent by e-mail to
comments@myreportlinks.com or to the address on the back cover.

Photo Credits: © Corel Corporation, pp. 1 (background), 3; Courtesy of
America's Story, The Library of Congress, p. 35; Courtesy of American Memory,
The Library of Congress, pp. 30, 33; Courtesy of Encyclopedia Americana, p. 41;
Courtesy of MyReportsLinks.com Books, p. 4; Courtesy of The American
Presidency, pp. 29, 36; Courtesy of The Herbert Hoover Presidential Library
and Museum, pp. 15, 17, 19, 22, 26; Courtesy of The Doughboy Center, p. 11;
The Herbert Hoover Presidential Library/Museum, pp. 23, 25, 27, 42; The
Library of Congress, p. 32; The National Archives and Records Administration,
p. 16; The United States Department of the Interior, p. 38.

Cover Photo: © Corel Corporation; The Herbert Hoover Presidential
Library/Museum.

NOV - - 2002

Contents

MyReportLinks.com Books
Great Books, Great Links, Great for Research!

MyReportLinks.com Books present the information you need to learn about your report subject. In addition, they show you where to go on the Internet for more information. The pre-evaluated Report Links, listed on **www.myreportlinks.com**, save hours of research time and link to dozens—even hundreds—of Web sites, source documents, and photos related to your report topic.

To Our Readers:
Each Report Link has been reviewed by our editors, who will work hard to keep only active and appropriate Internet addresses in our books and up to date on our Web site. However, the author and the Publisher have no control over, and assume no liability for, the material available on those Internet sites, or on other Web sites they may link to.

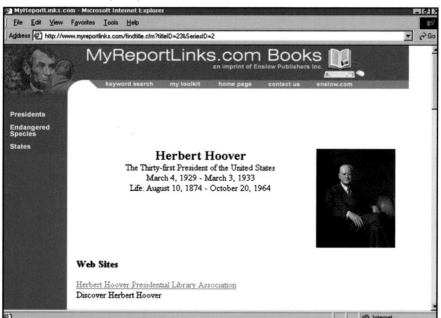

Access:
The Publisher will try to keep the Report Links that back up this book up to date on our Web site for three years from the book's first publication date. Please enter **PHO1131** if asked for a password.

Report Links

 The Internet sites described below can be accessed at
http://www.myreportlinks.com

*EDITOR'S CHOICE

▶ **Hoover Presidential Library Association**
The Herbert Hoover Presidential Library Association Web site provides
a wealth of information about Herbert Hoover. Here you will find
quotes, biographies, speeches, photos, and more.

Link to this Internet site from http://www.myreportlinks.com

*EDITOR'S CHOICE

▶ **Herbert Hoover: The Engineer President**
This site offers a detailed exploration of Herbert Hoover's life before,
during, and after his presidency, including his work as an engineer.

Link to this Internet site from http://www.myreportlinks.com

*EDITOR'S CHOICE

▶ **"Hoover Online!"**
Herbert Hoover Online is a comprehensive site about Herbert Hoover,
offering information about Hoover's life ranging from his boyhood in
Iowa to his career before and after the White House.

Link to this Internet site from http://www.myreportlinks.com

*EDITOR'S CHOICE

▶ **Herbert Hoover Presidential Library and Museum**
The National Archives and Records Administration offers a virtual tour
of the Herbert Hoover Presidential Library and Museum.

Link to this Internet site from http://www.myreportlinks.com

*EDITOR'S CHOICE

▶ **The American Presidency: Herbert Hoover**
Here you will find Herbert Hoover's inaugural address, some "quick
facts," and a detailed biography of Hoover.

Link to this Internet site from http://www.myreportlinks.com

*EDITOR'S CHOICE

▶ **"I Do Solemnly Swear..."**
This site contains memorabilia from Hoover's inaugural ceremony on
March 4, 1929. Here you will find the text of Hoover's address and a
handful of photos.

Link to this Internet site from http://www.myreportlinks.com

The Internet sites described below can be accessed at
http://www.myreportlinks.com

▶ **"Always Lend a Helping Hand"**
This essay discusses the Great Depression and, in particular, the extent to
which people blamed Hoover for the economic crisis.

Link to this Internet site from http://www.myreportlinks.com

▶ **The American Presidency: Charles Curtis**
This site provides a brief biography of Charles Curtis, Hoover's vice president.
Here you will learn about his life and career in politics.

Link to this Internet site from http://www.myreportlinks.com

▶ **The American Presidency: Lou Henry Hoover**
Here you will learn of Lou Hoover's global travels with her husband and about
their first meeting, in the geology department of Stanford University.

Link to this Internet site from http://www.myreportlinks.com

▶ **The Depths of Depression**
This site provides a description of the stock market crash in 1929 that
launched the Great Depression. Here you will find many photographs
documenting the times.

Link to this Internet site from http://www.myreportlinks.com

▶ **The Empire State Building Opens, May 1, 1931**
With the press of a button, President Herbert Hoover, from Washington
D.C., was the first to turn on the lights in the Empire State Building. This
site describes the building's opening.

Link to this Internet site from http://www.myreportlinks.com

▶ **Hawley-Smoot Tariff Act**
At this site you will find a brief description of the Hawley-Smoot Tariff Act,
which was signed by Herbert Hoover in 1930.

Link to this Internet site from http://www.myreportlinks.com

Report Links

The Internet sites described below can be accessed at
http://www.myreportlinks.com

▶Herbert Clark Hoover
This site provides facts and figures on Herbert Hoover. You will also
find presidential election results, a list of cabinet members, historical
documents, and other resources.

Link to this Internet site from http://www.myreportlinks.com

▶Herbert Hoover
This site provides a quick-reference guide to the life and political career
of Herbert Hoover, followed by a detailed biography.

Link to this Internet site from http://www.myreportlinks.com

▶Herbert Hoover
This site provides a number of facts about Herbert Hoover. You will
also find a letter written by Hoover and links to more information
about him.

Link to this Internet site from http://www.myreportlinks.com

▶Herbert Hoover
This site holds a brief description of Herbert Hoover and a portrait of
Hoover that was supposed to be on the cover of Time Magazine.

Link to this Internet site from http://www.myreportlinks.com

▶Herbert Hoover (1874–1964): Selections From the Archives of American Art
The Smithsonian Archives of American Art features two exhibits about
Herbert Hoover before his presidency.

Link to this Internet site from http://www.myreportlinks.com

▶Herbert Hoover Is Dead; Ex-President, 90, Served Country in Varied Fields
The *New York Times* obituary of Herbert Hoover appears on this Web
site. Hoover died on October 20, 1964, at the age of 90.

Link to this Internet site from http://www.myreportlinks.com

The Internet sites described below can be accessed at
http://www.myreportlinks.com

▶**Herbert Hoover: Inaugural Address, Monday, March 4, 1929**
Bartleby's vast electronic library holds Herbert Hoover's inaugural address,
which he delivered on March 4, 1929.

Link to this Internet site from http://www.myreportlinks.com

▶**The American President: "The American Way"**
At this site, four presidents are profiled for having had a vision for America.
Here you will learn about Hoover's vision and how the Depression thwarted
his plans.

Link to this Internet site from http://www.myreportlinks.com

▶**Hoover, Herbert Clark**
DiscoverySchool.com provides a profile of Herbert Hoover. Here you will
learn about Hoover's early life, political life, administration, and his life after
the presidency.

Link to this Internet site from http://www.myreportlinks.com

▶**Hoover Institution**
The Hoover Institution was founded in 1919 by Herbert Hoover. This
institution is dedicated to public policy research.

Link to this Internet site from http://www.myreportlinks.com

▶**Looking Back at the Crash of '29**
A columnist for the *New York Times* looks back at the 1929 stock
market crash. At this site, you can browse through the paper's coverage
of the collapse.

Link to this Internet site from http://www.myreportlinks.com

▶**Objects From the Presidency**
At this site you will find objects related to President Hoover and a description
of the era he lived in. You will also learn about the office of the presidency.

Link to this Internet site from http://www.myreportlinks.com

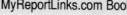
 The Internet sites described below can be accessed at
http://www.myreportlinks.com

▶**President Herbert Hoover**
Herbert Hoover came to the White House with an impressive record of
public service, having served his country as an engineer, administrator,
and cabinet member.

Link to this Internet site from http://www.myreportlinks.com

▶**President Hoover's Views on the Depression**
This Social Security Administration exhibit contains a letter from
President Hoover written shortly before leaving office. Here you will
learn Hoover's feelings about the Great Depression and the New Deal.

Link to this Internet site from http://www.myreportlinks.com

▶**The Sad Tale of the Bonus Marchers**
This site tells the story of World War I veterans who marched on
Washington to protest the government's hold on their bonuses.

Link to this Internet site from http://www.myreportlinks.com

▶**The White House: Herbert Hoover**
The official White House biography of Herbert Hoover provides a
brief overview of Hoover's political life and his rise to the presidency.

Link to this Internet site from http://www.myreportlinks.com

▶**The White House Historical Association**
The White House Historical Association Web site provides an extensive
history of the White House. You can also take a virtual tour of the
White House and learn about the presidents.

Link to this Internet site from http://www.myreportlinks.com

▶**The White House: Lou Henry Hoover**
The official White House biography of Lou Henry Hoover provides a
brief profile of the First Lady, the wife of the thirty-first president of
the United States.

Link to this Internet site from http://www.myreportlinks.com

Highlights

1874—*Aug. 10:* Herbert Hoover is born in a tiny three-room house in West Branch, Iowa.

1880—Herbert's father dies of typhoid fever.

1882—Herbert's mother dies of pneumonia.

1884—Herbert moves to Oregon to live with his uncle.

1895—Graduates from Stanford University with a degree in geology.

—Works for the United States Geological Survey and helps map the "gold belt" of California.

1897—*March*: Moves to western Australia and works as a gold-mining engineer.

1899—Moves to China, where he works as a mine manager and engineer for the Chinese government.

—*Feb. 10:* Marries Louise Henry.

1900—The Hoovers are trapped in Tientsin, China, during the Boxer Uprising.

1914—After World War I breaks out, Hoover heads a relief committee and helps stranded Americans to return home from Europe. He is also in charge of organizing food relief for Belgium.

1917—President Woodrow Wilson appoints Hoover U.S. food administrator to organize food rationing and food distribution so that supplies can be sent to the troops. After the war, Hoover establishes American Relief Administration to bring some 34 million tons of food and other supplies to Europeans in need.

1921–1922—Hoover serves as secretary of commerce in Harding and Coolidge administrations.

1928—Elected the thirty-first president of the United States.

1929—*March 4:* Hoover is inaugurated.

—*Oct. 29:* Stock market crashes; the Great Depression begins.

1932—Bonus Army marches on the White House, asking for Hoover's help. On July 28, he orders the U.S. Army to move the veterans.

1939—*Sept. 1:* World War II begins. During and after the war, Hoover works on getting food and supplies to Europe.

1944—His wife, Lou, dies.

1964—*Oct. 20:* Dies of cancer at the age of ninety.

The Bonus Army, 1932

In the summer of 1932, the city of Washington, D.C., was invaded—but not by any foreign power. A mostly peaceful group of twenty thousand unemployed veterans marched into the capital. Only fifteen years earlier they had fought

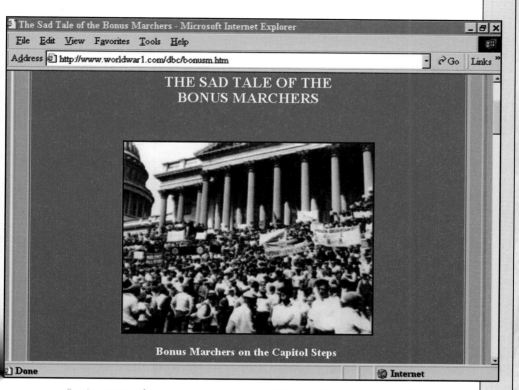

The Sad Tale of the Bonus Marchers - Microsoft Internet Explorer

File   Edit   View   Favorites   Tools   Help

Address http://www.worldwar1.com/dbc/bonusm.htm   Go   Links

THE SAD TALE OF THE BONUS MARCHERS

Bonus Marchers on the Capitol Steps

Done   Internet

▲ An army of some twenty thousand Bonus Marchers crowded the streets of Washington, D.C., during the summer of 1932. These unemployed World War I veterans were demanding the bonuses that the government had promised them. This photograph shows the Bonus Marchers on the steps of the Capitol.

for the United States in World War I, and now they were seeking the money that had been promised them.

America was suffering through a time called the Great Depression. In the years between 1929 and 1941, thousands of businesses failed, and millions of Americans were unemployed. In the United States in 1932, one out of four workers was out of work. People spent all of their savings just to survive. Even though most people did not want charity, they hoped their government and their president would help them in some way.

The World War I veterans were looking to their president, Herbert Hoover, for help. In 1924, the government had promised to reward them for their service to the nation by giving each veteran a bonus payment of about a thousand dollars. But the bonuses were not scheduled to be paid until 1945. The aging soldiers said they could not wait thirteen more years. They were unemployed now, their children were hungry now, and they needed the bonus now. When the government refused, thousands of veterans came to Washington to make their case in person. From all across America, in boxcars and old trucks or on foot, men came to join the "Bonus Army." From May through July of 1932, they camped out in parks in Washington, D.C.

The veterans hoped to see President Hoover, thinking that surely he would not turn them away. After all, they had fought to protect Europe, while Hoover had fought to feed it. Hoover had become famous for directing the delivery of food, clothes, and medical supplies to refugees and poor people in Europe. The veterans thought that this famous humanitarian would now help them in their time of need.

But Hoover refused to give the veterans what they wanted. He refused to pay the bonus early, as he had refused most requests for government aid to the millions of jobless Americans during the Depression. Hoover cared about their plight and desperately wanted to see the economy improve and put people back to work.

But Hoover believed in order and in an efficient and spare federal government. He felt that the government should not give money directly to people—that, to his way of thinking, was the role of private groups, like churches. If the government tried to help, Hoover believed, it would hurt the economy and hurt Americans more than help them.[1] And as president, Herbert Hoover acted to keep the Bonus Army from disrupting life in Washington by offering to pay the veterans' way home. Many accepted, but about two thousand remained in the city. On July 28, Hoover ordered the U.S. Army to join the police in moving the veterans.

The army swept down on the veterans, with soldiers on horseback and in tanks trying to break up the camp. Men with machine guns, tear gas, and bayonets forced veterans armed only with sticks and stones to retreat. No shots were fired, but the damage to Hoover's political future had already been done. The president announced that he had defeated mob rule and restored order and civil tranquility. But when the United States Army drove the Bonus Army from Washington, many people believed a great humanitarian had turned his back on the suffering of his own people.

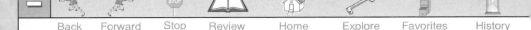
Growing Up, 1874–1895

When Herbert Hoover was born around midnight on August 10, 1874, his father, Jesse Hoover, was very proud. He told Herbert's aunt that he thought that his new little boy was just like President Ulysses S. Grant.[1] Many parents boast about their children, but Jesse Hoover's boasts turned out to be prophetic. Herbert Hoover would grow up to be a United States president.

▶ A Quaker Childhood in Iowa

Herbert was born in a tiny three-room house in the small town of West Branch, Iowa. Fewer than four hundred people lived in West Branch, and most of them were Quakers.[2] ("Quakers" is the popular name for members of the Religious Society of Friends.) Quakerism, founded in seventeenth-century England, is rooted in the Christian faith, but differs from other Christian groups in its emphasis on individual spirituality. Quakers have historically been opposed to war and have worked to promote peace through education. The Hoovers were Quakers, and like others of their faith, they dressed simply, attended Quaker meetings, and refrained from drinking or smoking.

In many ways, Herbert Hoover's life was a lot like the lives of other small-town children. Everyone called him "Herbie." He attended the local school. And he played with his older brother, Theodore, and his younger sister, May. Herbie's father, Jesse, was a blacksmith. He made

Tools   Search   Notes   Discuss   Go!

GALLERY ONE: Years of Adventure - Microsoft Internet Explorer

File   Edit   View   Favorites   Tools   Help   Links »

Address ⟨🔲⟩ http://hoover.nara.gov/gallery/Hooverstory/gallery01/gallery01.html   ⌄ ⌀Go

An Iowa Boyhood

I carry the brand of Iowa," said Herbert Hoover, recalling the experience of a five-year-old, barefoot boy stepping on a hot iron in his father's blacksmith shop. In many ways Hoover never shed the stamp of his Quaker upbringing in West Branch, Iowa, where he was born August 10, 1874. His father, Jesse, combined Quaker piety with a very American desire to get ahead in the world. Jesse's wife Hulda was a sweet-faced, devout woman who took Herbert, his brother Theodore and sister May to the unheated Meetinghouse, where Bert sat quietly, sometimes for hours, as his elders waited for the Quaker Inner Light to move them to speak.

The boy's early reading was limited to the Bible, schoolbooks, "certain novels showing the huge danger of Demon Rum" and a pirated copy of the "Youth's Companion." Young Bert enjoyed sledding on frosty winter nights, an activity his Aunt Hannah thought Godless. In the summer, he picked potato bugs to earn money for Fourth of July firecrackers.

1877-2: Herbert Hoover at age three, West Branch, 1877. (unknown copyright)

🛈 Internet

Herbert Hoover was born in a tiny three-room cottage in West Branch, Iowa, on August 10, 1874. This photograph shows him at three years of age.

horseshoes and tools out of iron. One day, Herbie was watching his father boil tar. When his father was not looking, Herbie put a burning stick in the tar to see what would happen. He got his answer when clouds of smoke came pouring out—so much smoke that the fire department and the townspeople came to see. Herbie kept it a secret that he had started the fire until he had grown up.

When Herbie was three, his father started a business that sold farm equipment. Soon the family had more money and moved to a bigger house. But the easy times did not last long.

▲ Remaining true to his childhood roots, Herbert Hoover as president continued to take pleasure in simple things, like fishing.

▶ Hard Times for the Hoovers

When Herbie was only six years old, Jesse Hoover died of typhoid fever. His father's death made things difficult for his mother, Huldah. To support her family, she sewed clothes for other people and rented out a room in the Hoover house. As soon as the children were old enough, they worked to help earn money for the family. Herbie picked strawberries in the summer, and he and Theodore collected old iron to sell. When there was time for play, playing outside was Herbie's favorite thing to do.[3] In West Branch, he liked to sled in the winter and fish in the summer. He and his brother hunted pigeons and other birds and also trapped rabbits.

Herbie's mother, a very religious woman, became a Quaker minister, and her ministry often called for her to travel. On those occasions, Herbie and his brother and sister stayed with relatives. One such extended visit took

Herbie to his uncle's family, who lived on the Osage Indian reservation in Indian Territory. It was quite an adventure for Herbie, who played with the Osage children. They taught him how to hunt with a bow and arrow, and they fished together. Herbie spent nearly nine months on the reservation.

Tragedy again touched the Hoover family. When Herbie was eight, his mother died of pneumonia. Now the Hoover children were orphans, and they were sent to live with different relatives, as no one could afford to take all three children. Herbie lived with relatives until he was grown up.

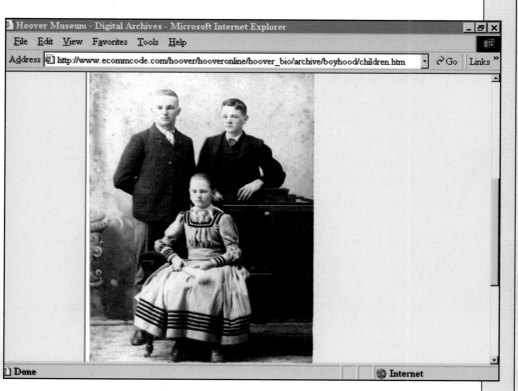

Hoover Museum - Digital Archives - Microsoft Internet Explorer

File   Edit   View   Favorites   Tools   Help

Address http://www.ecommcode.com/hoover/hooveronline/hoover_bio/archive/boyhood/children.htm   Go   Links

Done   Internet

▲ *This photograph was taken in 1888, when Hoover and his brother and sister were reunited in Salem, Oregon. After the death of their mother, the Hoover children were sent to live with different relatives.*

First, Herbie went to live with an uncle and his family on a farm near West Branch. Herbie helped with the farm work—feeding hogs, plowing, and planting and harvesting corn and wheat. The family chopped wood to use as fuel, made their own soap, and grew their own food.

▶ Out West

In 1884, ten-year-old Herbie went to live with another uncle, who loved in Oregon. West Branch was the only place Herbie had known. Though he was sad to leave his family and friends, he was also excited about the train trip west across the Rocky Mountains.[4]

Oregon was full of new experiences for Herbie. His uncle, Henry John Minthorn, was a country doctor and was in charge of a Quaker school. Herbie traveled with him when he made house calls and thus learned a lot about medicine and the human body. He also took care of the family's horses and milked their cow.

When Herbie was fifteen, he moved with the Minthorns to Salem, Oregon. His uncle started a business buying and selling land. Herbie stopped going to school to work in his uncle's office. He never went to high school—his education during those years was what he learned at work or on his own. He learned to type, to do accounting, and to write advertisements. He also read geometry and geology books in his free time. Herbie was shy and quiet; he never tried to be the center of attention. But the people who knew him best knew that he was intelligent and serious.[5]

Herbert Hoover eventually decided that he needed more of a formal education, so he took night classes at a business school. His dream was to go to college to study engineering, and Stanford University was a new college in

California that had a good engineering program. Though Hoover studied hard, he failed to pass Stanford's entrance exam. He was lucky, though. Stanford gave him a second chance to take the test, and when he passed, he was admitted to the new university.

Life at College

Herbert started his studies at Stanford when he was only seventeen. Always willing to work hard, he took jobs to pay for college. He delivered newspapers, delivered clean clothes for a laundry company, and worked in an office. He also found time to be active in student government.

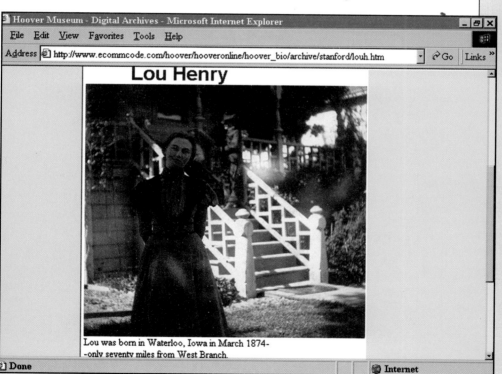

Hoover Museum - Digital Archives - Microsoft Internet Explorer

File   Edit   View   Favorites   Tools   Help

Address http://www.ecommcode.com/hoover/hooveronline/hoover_bio/archive/stanford/louh.htm   Go   Links

Lou Henry

Lou was born in Waterloo, Iowa in March 1874--only seventy miles from West Branch.

Done   Internet

Herbert Hoover met Louise "Lou" Henry at Stanford University, where both were studying geology. They became friends and were married after Lou's graduation, in 1899.

Even as a college student, Herbert Hoover was still very shy and didn't have many friends. One of his classmates and friends was Louise Henry, known to her friends as "Lou." Like Herbert, Lou was studying geology—the scientific study of the earth, its history, and the materials that make it up. She was the first woman to major in geology at the university. Herbert also loved geology, and was good at it. He was so good that a professor hired him to help make maps of the geology of mountains in Arkansas, California, and Nevada. Once Herbert walked more than eighty miles to get to the mountains to do his work. After Herbert Hoover graduated from Stanford in 1895, he looked for work as a geologist.

Chapter 3

Engineer and Businessman, 1896–1928

In the summer of 1895, after graduating from college, Hoover went to work for the United States Geological Survey. He helped map the "gold belt" of California, a part of the state in which there were many gold mines. Following that, he began working as a gold miner in Nevada City, California. Hoover pushed carts of gold ore in the mine, deep underground. It was hard, dirty work, moving heavy carts around in a dark, damp tunnel.

What he wanted was to be a mining engineer, able to tell miners where and how to dig. After a couple of months, he found a job in San Francisco working as a typist in the office of a mining company. The owner saw that Hoover had potential and soon promoted him. Hoover then traveled to Arizona, Nevada, and Wyoming to study the company's mines. It was a happy time for him—he enjoyed his work, and he also shared a house with his brother, his sister, and a cousin. They went on drives and picnics. And Herbert Hoover often spent the rest of his free time at Stanford University, visiting Louise Henry.[1]

▶ From California to Australia

In March 1897, Hoover got a job as a mining engineer for some gold mines in western Australia. It was a big job for such a young man—he was only twenty-two years old. But it would mark the beginning of a brilliant career. His work helped make one of the gold mines a great success— by making the mine more efficient, he made the mine

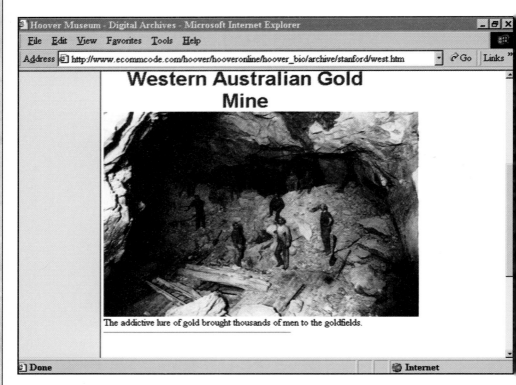

Western Australian Gold Mine

The addictive lure of gold brought thousands of men to the goldfields.

Hoover traveled all over the world working as a mining engineer. In 1897, he was hired to work in the gold mines of western Australia.

owners wealthy. And though Herbert Hoover was far from home, he continued to stay in touch with Lou Henry, who was still studying at Stanford. (She would graduate in 1899.)

The Hoovers in China and Around the World

In 1899, Hoover took a new job as a mine manager and engineer for the Chinese government. The day he accepted the job, he sent a telegram to Lou Henry, asking her to marry him. She sent a telegram back to say she would. He took a boat back to America, and the couple were married on February 10. The next day they left for China.

Herbert and Lou Hoover traveled all over the Chinese empire, inspecting and improving mines. Their travels took them to the Gobi Desert, Tibet, Mongolia, and many other places. Herbert learned a little Chinese, and Lou learned a lot. With her own knowledge of geology and her fluency in Chinese, she played an important part in her husband's work.

In 1900, a group of Chinese who believed that outsiders controlled too much of China's business and government grew angry with the Europeans and Americans in China. They did not want foreigners teaching their religion in China either. These Chinese militants were called "Boxers" by English speakers because their combat techniques resembled boxing moves. The rebellion against foreigners in China thus became known as the Boxer Uprising. As Americans living and working in China in 1900, the Hoovers were in great danger. Foreigners were being

▲ This photo was taken from one of Hoover's personal scrapbooks. While living in China during the Boxer Uprising, the Hoovers were trapped in Tientsin. "Machine guns on our next corner" were the words Hoover used to describe the climate of fear the Hoovers endured. This photo shows Lou Hoover standing next to a cannon.

attacked in their homes—once a cannonball even crashed into the Hoovers' house. For a time, the Hoovers were trapped in the city of Tientsin. An international force was sent into China to restore order and protect those under attack, and the fighting soon ceased.

The Hoovers stayed in China for two years and then traveled to Australia, Burma, South Africa, England, and Russia, among other places, where Herbert Hoover set up new mines and improved old ones. Lou Hoover traveled with her husband, and over those years gave birth to two sons: Herbert, Jr., was born in 1903, and Allan was born in 1907.

▶ Feeding the Hungry and Rising to Fame

By 1914, Herbert Hoover had become a wealthy man, mostly from profits from a silver mine in Burma. He had accumulated about 4 million dollars in money and property. His work as an engineer was notable, but it was his work during World War I that made him famous.

Hoover was in London when World War I broke out in Europe in the summer of 1914. The Central Powers, Germany, the Austro-Hungarian Empire, and Turkey, were fighting England, France, and Russia, known as the Allies. Other countries would become involved in the fighting. The United States had not yet entered the war, so the Americans living in Europe were caught in the middle. Many didn't have enough money to remain in Europe, but it was too dangerous for them to return home because German submarines were attacking ships.

The U.S. Embassy in London asked Hoover if he would help them, so he set up the American Relief Committee with some friends. They used government money and private donations to feed the nearly 120,000

▲ *Belgium suffered greatly from Nazi occupation during World War I. Herbert Hoover created the Commission for the Relief of Belgium, which obtained and distributed much-needed food and clothing to the war-ravaged people of that country.*

stranded Americans and eventually send them home safely. But Americans were not the only ones who needed help in war-torn Europe.

By August of 1914, Germany had taken over the small country of Belgium. Soon the Belgian people did not have enough food because the German army took it to feed German troops. Hoover created the Commission for the Relief of Belgium and, through private donations, was able to distribute food, clothing, and other supplies to the people of Belgium.

▶ Hero at Home and Abroad

On April 6, 1917, the United States entered World War I by declaring war on Germany and joining England and France as an ally. President Woodrow Wilson knew it would take a lot of food to feed the armies of the United

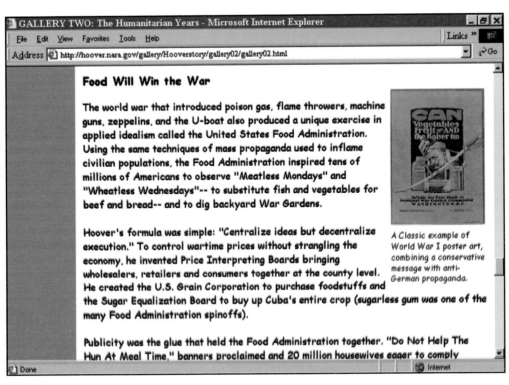

GALLERY TWO: The Humanitarian Years - Microsoft Internet Explorer

File   Edit   View   Favorites   Tools   Help   Links »

Address   http://hoover.nara.gov/gallery/Hooverstory/gallery02/gallery02.html   Go

Food Will Win the War

The world war that introduced poison gas, flame throwers, machine guns, zeppelins, and the U-boat also produced a unique exercise in applied idealism called the United States Food Administration. Using the same techniques of mass propaganda used to inflame civilian populations, the Food Administration inspired tens of millions of Americans to observe "Meatless Mondays" and "Wheatless Wednesdays"-- to substitute fish and vegetables for beef and bread-- and to dig backyard War Gardens.

Hoover's formula was simple: "Centralize ideas but decentralize execution." To control wartime prices without strangling the economy, he invented Price Interpreting Boards bringing wholesalers, retailers and consumers together at the county level. He created the U.S. Grain Corporation to purchase foodstuffs and the Sugar Equalization Board to buy up Cuba's entire crop (sugarless gum was one of the many Food Administration spinoffs).

Publicity was the glue that held the Food Administration together. "Do Not Help The Hun At Meal Time," banners proclaimed and 20 million housewives eager to comply

A Classic example of World War I poster art, combining a conservative message with anti-German propaganda.

Done   Internet

△ *During World War I, Hoover encouraged Americans to conserve wheat, meat, sugar, and fat so that food products could be sent to American troops. "Meatless, wheatless, sweetless, heatless" became a popular slogan during the war.*

States and its allies. Wilson was aware of Hoover's success in getting food to Belgium, so he asked Hoover to take charge of getting food to the Allied armies by appointing him the U.S. food administrator in 1917. In that position, Hoover succeeded in convincing Americans at home to consume less so that food could be sent to the troops overseas. By the time the fighting ended, in 1918, Hoover was a hero in Europe and America. He had provided America and its allies with the basic supplies that had helped them to win the war.

But even after the fighting ceased, the people of Europe were still in great need of help. Many were left with very little. At the request of Allied leaders, Hoover established the American Relief Administration and started distributing food and supplies to the people who needed them. The more than 34 million tons of supplies that reached the people of Europe in the years following World War I helped to save millions of lives.

Throughout the war years, one fact about Hoover that attracted a lot of attention was his refusal to accept any pay for his work helping people. For years, he worked as a volunteer to serve others. Throughout his political career, Herbert Hoover refused any pay for his service.

▲ Herbert Hoover continued his relief efforts in Europe after the United States entered World War I. President Woodrow Wilson appointed Hoover food administrator in 1917, and after the war, Hoover took charge of the American Relief Administration, seeing that food and other supplies reached the people in Europe who so greatly needed them.

▶ Entering Politics

Hoover's popularity had become so great that some Americans talked about electing him president in 1920. He was popular among Republicans and Democrats alike. But Hoover did not campaign for the office, and Warren G. Harding, a Republican, was elected president in 1920. Harding appointed Hoover secretary of commerce. When Harding died in office and the vice president, Calvin Coolidge, became president, Coolidge kept Hoover on as secretary of commerce.

Hoover believed that the government should cooperate with businesses.[2] He often asked business owners to help decide what the government should do, and he used the government to collect the information that businesses needed. He created government agencies to help develop the new radio and airline industries.

Many Americans admired him for his accomplishments as commerce secretary. Businesses and wealthy people were certainly profiting by making more money than ever before. When Hoover decided to run for president in the election of 1928, he won the support of the Republican Party, which chose him as its candidate.

▶ Election of 1928

Hoover's opponent was Al Smith, the Democratic candidate and the governor of New York. The two men held very different opinions, and they appealed to different voters. Generally, people who approved of Prohibition—which had made it illegal to make, sell, or distribute alcoholic beverages—supported Hoover, while those who wanted to overturn the 1920 amendment that brought about Prohibition supported Smith. Voters in small towns mostly

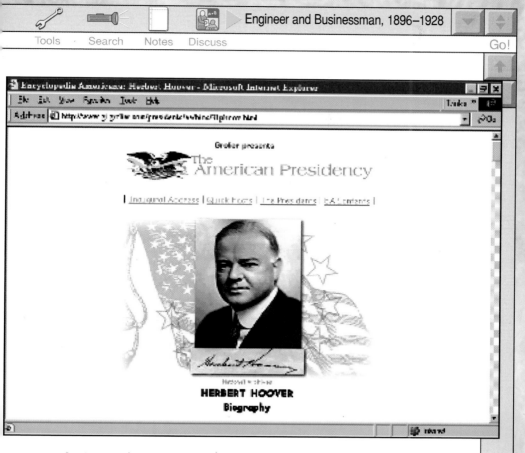

Encyclopedia Americana: Herbert Hoover - Microsoft Internet Explorer

File Edit View Favorites Tools Help

Links

Address http://www.grolier.com/presidents/ea/bios/31phoov.html   Go

Grolier presents

The American Presidency

| Inaugural Address | Quick Facts | The Presidents | EA Contents |

Herbert Hoover

HERBERT HOOVER
Biography

As president, Hoover had to cope with one of the worst crises in American history—the Great Depression. His noteworthy efforts to feed millions during the two world wars are often overshadowed by memories of the country's suffering in the 1930s.

supported Hoover, while voters in cities mostly supported Smith. And Al Smith was a Roman Catholic, and no Roman Catholic had ever been elected president. But most of all, a majority of voters wanted businesses to continue doing well. They thought Hoover would do that, so they voted for him.

Hoover won the presidential election of 1928 by capturing the vote in forty of the forty-eight states. It was an amazing victory. Jesse Hoover had been right all those years ago. Like General Ulysses S. Grant, Herbert Hoover had become president.

Chapter 4

Presiding Over Disaster, 1929–1933

On March 4, 1929, Herbert Hoover mounted the steps of the United States Capitol building. He placed his hand on a Bible and swore to uphold the Constitution. Then he spoke to the thousands of Americans who had come to see him take the oath of office. On that day, he was full of

This photograph was taken during Hoover's inauguration, on March 4, 1929. On that day, he stated that he had "no fear for the future of our country." Less than a year later, the stock market crashed, and Hoover's administration was blamed for the Great Depression.

optimism. "I have no fear for the future of our country," he said. "It is bright with hope."[1]

There were already serious problems in the country, however. Farmers had been having a very hard time all through the 1920s. The amount of money they were earning for their crops kept going down while the cost of farming supplies and equipment kept going up. It got harder for farmers to make any money from farming.

One of the first things that Hoover did as president was to convince Congress to pass a law called the Agricultural Marketing Act. It helped farmers set up cooperatives, in which groups of farmers who all grow the same crops work together to get the best prices for their products. There were already cooperatives in America, but Hoover wanted to create more. They were a way, he said, of helping people help themselves.[2] And the cooperatives helped a little, at first. Hoover encouraged other businesses to set up similar groups. Pretty soon, though, America's economic problems were so great that the cooperatives and business groups could not help much.

The Crash

In late October 1929, only seven months into Hoover's presidency, the price of stocks in the stock market fell very fast, with investors losing a lot of money. The worst came on October 29, when stock prices fell so fast that the newspapers called it a "crash." Billions of dollars were lost on the market that day. The crash of 1929 marked the beginning of a period that would come to be known as the Great Depression, and it would affect not only the United States but also the entire world for at least a decade.

The Great Depression began in 1929 and lasted until 1941. During those years, businesses and farmers and

▲ The Great Depression began only seven months after Hoover became president, and it would continue after he left office. Many Americans living through the Depression felt that Hoover's passive policies did little to address their suffering, as this cartoon shows.

everyday people all across the world had a terrible time making enough money to buy even basic things like food and medicine. Millions lost their jobs or had their wages reduced. That meant they could not buy products from businesses, and businesses in turn could not sell their products. Since businesses made less money, they had to fire employees or pay them less. Thus, people could not afford to buy the products that businesses were trying to sell, and the vicious cycle continued. It left workers jobless, families homeless, farmers hungry, banks closed, and businesses ruined.

Herbert Hoover did not bring about the Depression, but he was partly responsible for how badly Americans suffered during it. The Depression was not caused by one single event. But one reason it was so severe and lasted so long was that banks and the stock market in the early 1920s did not follow safe practices. Hoover, who had been secretary of commerce during those years, had worked hard to keep businesses strong. But although he had worried about some of these dangerous practices, he did little to stop them.

American Memory Digital Item Display - fsa2000000930/PP - Microsoft Internet Explorer

File   Edit   View   Favorites   Tools   Help

Address UMBER+@band(fsa+8b31768))+@field(COLLID+fsa)):displayType=1.m856sd=fsa.m856sf=   Go   Links

Done   Internet

▲This photograph, taken in California in 1937, when Franklin Roosevelt was president, shows people waiting to get their relief checks from the government. Many who had lost their jobs and could not find work during the Depression felt Hoover's administration had done little to ease their suffering.

Hoover Holds the Line

At first, neither Hoover nor the American people knew how serious the Depression was or how long it would last. In the spring of 1930, Hoover told Americans not to worry and promised them that things would get better soon.[3] But things got worse instead. That spring, 4 million Americans were unemployed. At the same time, drought hit farmers in the southern Great Plains states. In some places, the soil was so dry that the wind blew it away in clouds of dust. The region became known as the Dust Bowl. Since farming was impossible there, families had to leave their land and look for work in other states, but there was very little work available.

Americans looked to the president for a solution, expecting him to take dramatic action. But Hoover remembered that after World War I, there had been a depression. The government had done little to intervene then, and that depression had ended as businesses grew and the country prospered. Hoover thought the same thing would happen in the 1930s.[4] But the Great Depression kept growing worse.

In 1930, Congress decided to spend $750 million on construction projects. The government hired men to build public buildings and highways and to improve harbors. Many Americans thought that the government should spend more and create more jobs, but Hoover disagreed. He thought money would be wasted on building things the nation did not really need. His decision made many Americans angry.[5]

They got even angrier when Hoover refused to allow the government to give money directly to the American people who were neediest. Then, in July 1932, he directed the U.S. Army to remove the Bonus Army marchers from

page 1 of 2 NEXT

▲ On May 1, 1931, Hoover pushed a button in Washington, D.C., and lit up the world's tallest skyscraper at the time, the Empire State Building, in New York City.

Washington. That event led many people to believe that Hoover just did not care about poor people's problems.[6]

Hoover did care, but he disagreed with those who thought the government should give money directly to people or should take action to help investors. He especially disagreed with those who said that the government should become involved in business by telling companies not to fire people or not to lower people's pay. Hoover thought businesses should form groups, like the farm cooperatives that had been established through the Agricultural Marketing Act. He believed that those groups

should decide to do things that would make the economy work better.[7]

Hoover did believe, however, that government had to help businesses so that they could hire more people and pay them more. So he created the Reconstruction Finance Corporation, which lent money to railroads, banks, and insurance companies and eventually to other businesses. Hoover's defense was that he had to help these institutions if they were to stay in business. But many Americans saw this action by Hoover as just helping rich people—those who owned the banks and railroads—instead of helping poor people.[8]

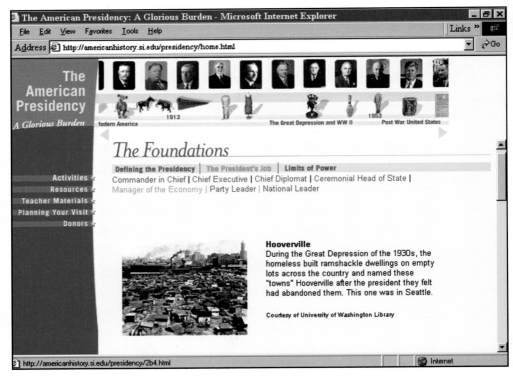

The American Presidency: A Glorious Burden - Microsoft Internet Explorer

File Edit View Favorites Tools Help   Links »

Address http://americanhistory.si.edu/presidency/home.html   Go

The American Presidency
A Glorious Burden

1913   The Great Depression and WW II   1953   Post War United States

Modern America

The Foundations

Defining the Presidency | The President's Job | **Limits of Power**
Commander in Chief | Chief Executive | Chief Diplomat | Ceremonial Head of State |
Manager of the Economy | Party Leader | National Leader

Activities
Resources
Teacher Materials
Planning Your Visit
Donors

Hooverville
During the Great Depression of the 1930s, the homeless built ramshackle dwellings on empty lots across the country and named these "towns" Hooverville after the president they felt had abandoned them. This one was in Seattle.

Courtesy of University of Washington Library

http://americanhistory.si.edu/presidency/2b4.html   Internet

During the Great Depression of the 1930s, Americans began calling the slums in which they lived "Hoovervilles" because they blamed the president for their poor living conditions.

Hoover's actions did little to slow the Depression, and they may have made it worse. They certainly made him unpopular.[9] People coined new terms to describe their living conditions that showed they blamed Hoover for their problems. During the Depression, the huts and tents people lived in because they had lost their homes became known as "Hoovervilles." A "Hoover hog" was a rabbit, a squirrel, or another small, wild animal that was caught for food because there was little else to eat. Newspapers that homeless people covered themselves with as they slept were called "Hoover blankets." Hoover heard these terms. His reserved manner did little to silence his critics. And he realized it was not going to be easy for him to get reelected in 1932.[10]

▶ The Election of 1932

Hoover's opponent in the 1932 presidential election was Franklin Delano Roosevelt, a Democrat, who accused Hoover of doing almost nothing to lift America out of the Depression. Roosevelt promised to get help to all those Americans who needed it. He said he would reform the stock market so that there would not be another crash, and he told farmers he would help them get good prices for their products. Roosevelt promised all of these things and more in his campaign. And he promised he would not spend more money than the government could afford.

Hoover traveled across the country, trying to convince the American people that the economy in 1932 was improving and that he was the one who would get America out of the Depression. He criticized Roosevelt's ideas, saying they would ruin American business and would cost too much money.

But more voters believed Roosevelt. On November 8, 1932, Herbert Hoover lost the presidency to Franklin

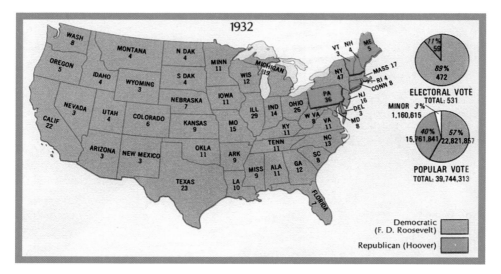

1932

ELECTORAL VOTE
TOTAL: 531

11%
59

89%
472

POPULAR VOTE
TOTAL: 39,744,313

MINOR 3%
1,160,615

40%
15,761,841

57%
22,821,857

Democratic
(F. D. Roosevelt)

Republican (Hoover)

▲ *This map shows how lopsided Roosevelt's victory was in the presidential election of 1932. FDR carried forty-two states to Hoover's six. Hoover's defeat was one of the worst in American history.*

Delano Roosevelt in one of the worst election defeats in American history. Hoover carried only six states, while Roosevelt won in forty-two.

Hoover's term lasted until March 4, 1933, but he was so unpopular that he accomplished very little in his last days as president. He had failed to win the confidence of the American people, and he could not convince Congress to pass the laws he wanted. Roosevelt would not even meet with him to discuss the transition of government. Hoover's last days in the White House were those of a president with very little power.

Chapter 5

The Later Years, 1933–1964

The years following his presidency were productive ones for Herbert Hoover. Though Hoover never officially ran for office again, he remained politically active. His talents at getting and distributing food to people during and after wartime would again be put to use. And he continued to call for a small and efficient government.

The man who succeeded Herbert Hoover as president had a much different view of what government should be, and a much easier time working with Congress. Franklin Delano Roosevelt got Congress to create many laws and programs. Some gave money directly to the people who needed it. Others helped safeguard against another depression. Roosevelt believed that the government was justified in making rules that forced businesses to treat American workers better.

Hoover thought all of these measures were dangerous and wrong, and he feared that Roosevelt's policies would weaken the American economy. But what Hoover liked least about Roosevelt's policies was that they told businesses what to do. He thought that Roosevelt was making America into a Communist country like the Soviet Union, and Hoover hated communism.[1]

Hoover tried to get the Republican Party to support him as its presidential candidate in the 1940 election even though he had said he would never run again. The party, however, nominated another man, Wendell Wilkie.[2]

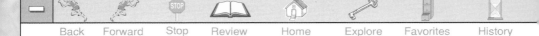

▶ War and Hunger, Again

In the 1930s, war was breaking out in Asia, Africa, and Europe. Japan invaded its neighbors in Asia and in the Pacific Ocean islands. Italy defeated the African nation of Ethiopia. Germany was especially aggressive. Its leader, Adolf Hitler, had built up a strong military and had expanded Germany by taking over Austria. In 1938, Nazi Germany invaded the Sudetenland, a region in western Czechoslovakia where many Germans lived. But Hitler did not stop there. The following year, Germany took control of the rest of that country and then invaded Poland.

Hoover was firm in his belief that America should stay out of the war. Like many Americans, Hoover was against sending American soldiers to other countries.[3] Instead, he worked to send food and supplies to the needy, as he had in World War I. He organized aid for people in Poland, Finland, Belgium, and other countries that the Nazis invaded. But when Japan bombed Pearl Harbor in December 1941, Hoover changed his mind—he finally supported America getting into the war.[4]

When the war ended, in 1945, millions of people around the world were hungry. Many homes and farms had been destroyed. In 1946, President Harry Truman (who had succeeded Roosevelt as president following his death) appointed Hoover the coordinator of the Food Supply for World Famine, to help get food to those who needed it. Hoover traveled around the world, convincing countries to consume less food so that it could be sent to places where people were most in need of it. In many of those countries, he was welcomed as a hero. He had helped to keep millions of people from starving during and after World War I. Now his efforts following World War II

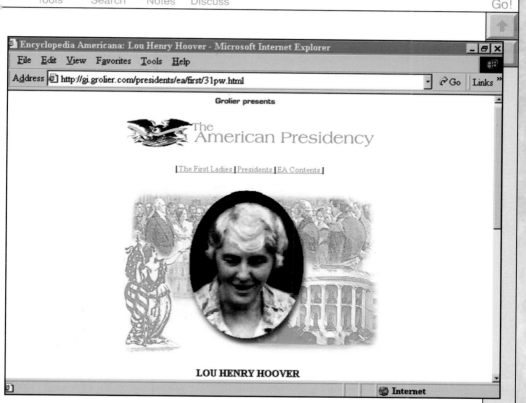

Grolier presents

The American Presidency

[The First Ladies][Presidents][EA Contents]

LOU HENRY HOOVER

▲ During her life, Louise "Lou" Henry was, among other things, a geologist, wife, mother, president of the Girl Scouts of America, and First Lady. Herbert Hoover described his wife as "a symbol of everything wholesome in American life."

helped avert more tragedy by bringing food to the world's people once again.

But during the war, Hoover suffered a personal tragedy. On January 7, 1944, Hoover found his wife, Lou, collapsed on the floor. She had died from a heart attack. The couple had been married for forty-five years. They had always worked as a team throughout Hoover's career in mine engineering, in politics, and in getting food to hungry people around the world. Now, Herbert Hoover had to do this work alone.

▶ Rebuilding Europe and Fighting Communism

In the years following World War II, President Truman again asked Herbert Hoover to step forward and help Germany and Austria to rebuild their economies. Many people feared that if Germany were given assistance, it would become strong enough to build up its military and begin another war. Hoover, however, disagreed. He thought that the real danger in Europe came from the Soviet Union and communism. Hoover wanted Germany to be given a chance to grow into a wealthy and powerful country again so that it would not turn to communism and would protect Europe from the Soviet Union. Hoover

▲ *This photograph of Herbert Hoover, Henry Ford, Thomas Edison, and Harvey Firestone was taken at a party celebrating Edison's eighty-second birthday, on February 11, 1929. This gathering included some of the most influential men of the twentieth century—and captures Hoover at what must have been a happy time for him, just before his grueling days as president began.*

therefore supported the Marshall Plan, which helped West Germany and many other European countries rebuild after the war.[5]

In 1947, Truman asked Hoover to become the chairman of a commission investigating the workings of government. In 1954, President Dwight Eisenhower asked Hoover to do the same thing. In both instances, Hoover and his team made suggestions on how government could work more efficiently and spend less money.

Eighty and Beyond

Ever since he had been a boy on a farm in Iowa, Herbert Hoover had worked hard. In the last years of his life, he continued to work. He supported conservative politicians, spoke on the dangers of communism, and wrote books on politics. He raised money for the Boys Clubs of America. At the age of eighty-six, he reported that he still worked ten hours every day.[6] It seemed as if time would never catch up with the ex-president.

But in 1962, Hoover was finally forced to slow down. Doctors told him that he had cancer, and he fought the disease for two years. Finally, though, on October 20, 1964, Herbert Hoover died, at the age of ninety. He was buried in West Branch, just a few steps away from the house where he had been born.

Hoover's Legacy

Most presidents are known for what they do while they are in office. That, however, cannot be said of Herbert Hoover. His policies as president did not last because Roosevelt made great changes once he succeeded Hoover—changes that are considered to have helped the country finally grow out of the Depression. And Hoover will forever be associated

with the Depression, since it began during his term and did not end until after he had left office.

Herbert Hoover's greatest legacy lies in what he accomplished before and after his presidency. During and after World War I and World War II, he helped feed millions of people around the world. He further helped the countries of Europe that had been so devastated by war to rebuild afterward. His relief efforts allowed the children in those countries to live and to grow up strong. Their very lives are testimony to Hoover's achievements.

Chapter Notes

Chapter 1. The Bonus Army, 1932

1. Joan Hoff Wilson, *Herbert Hoover: Forgotten Progressive* (Boston: Little, Brown & Co., 1975), pp. 129–130.

Chapter 2. Growing Up, 1874–1895

1. Will Irwin, *Herbert Hoover: A Reminiscent Biography* (New York: The Century Co., 1928), p. 7.

2. George H. Nash, *The Life of Herbert Hoover: The Engineer, 1874–1914* (New York: W.W. Norton & Co., 1983), p. 5.

3. Eugene Lyons, *Herbert Hoover: A Biography* (Garden City, N.J.: Doubleday & Co., 1964), p. 15.

4. Ibid., p. 17.

5. Irwin, pp. 27–30.

Chapter 3. Engineer and Businessman, 1896–1928

1. George H. Nash, *The Life of Herbert Hoover: The Engineer, 1874–1914* (New York: W.W. Norton & Co., 1983), pp. 49–50.

2. Joan Hoff Wilson, *Herbert Hoover: Forgotten Progressive* (Boston: Little, Brown & Co., 1975), p. 83.

Chapter 4. Presiding Over Disaster, 1929–1933

1. Herbert Hoover, *The State Papers and Other Public Writings of Herbert Hoover* (New York: Doubleday, Doran & Co., 1934), p. 12.

2. Edgar Eugene Robinson and Vaughn Davis Bornet, *Herbert Hoover: President of the United States* (Stanford, Calif.: Hoover Institution Press, 1975), pp. 71–75.

3. William A. DeGregorio, *The Complete Book of U.S. Presidents* (New York: Wings Books, 1997), p. 473.

4. Joan Hoff Wilson, *Herbert Hoover: Forgotten Progressive* (Boston: Little, Brown & Co., 1975), p. 146.

5. Ibid., pp. 150–151.

6. Robinson, pp. 236–237.

7. Paul Keith Conkin, *The New Deal*, 3rd ed. (Arlington Heights, Ill.: Harlan Davidson, 1992), pp. 26–27.

8. Frederick Lewis Allen, *Since Yesterday: The 1930s in America, September 3, 1929–September 3, 1939* (New York: Harper & Row, 1972), p. 42.

9. Elliot A. Rosen, *Hoover, Roosevelt and the Brains Trust: From Depression to New Deal* (New York: Columbia University Press, 1977), p. 53.

10. Wilson, p. 142.

Chapter 5. The Later Years, 1933–1964

1. Joan Hoff Wilson, *Herbert Hoover: Forgotten Progressive* (Boston: Little, Brown & Co., 1975), p. 236.

2. Gary Dean Best, *Herbert Hoover: The Postpresidential Years: 1933–1964*, vol. 1 (Stanford, Calif.: Hoover Institution Press, 1983), pp. 154–165.

3. Ibid., p. 127.

4. Eugene Lyons, *Herbert Hoover: A Biography* (Garden City, N.J.: Doubleday & Co., 1964), pp. 362, 370.

5. Best, pp. 319–322.

6. Ibid., p. 417.

Further Reading

Barber, William J. *From New Era to New Deal: Herbert Hoover, the Economists and American Economic Policy, 1921–1933.* New York: Cambridge University Press, 1989.

Clinton, Susan. *Herbert Hoover: Thirty-first President of the United States.* Danbury, Conn.: Children's Press, 1988.

Fausold, Martin L. *The Presidency of Herbert C. Hoover.* Lawrence, Kans.: University Press of Kansas, 1985.

Hilton, Suzanne. *The World of Young Herbert Hoover.* New York: Walker & Company, 1987.

Holford, David M. *Herbert Hoover.* Berkeley Heights, NJ: Enslow Publishers, Inc., 1999.

Joseph, Paul. *Herbert Hoover.* Minneapolis, Minn.: ABDO Publishing Company, 2001.

Nash, George H. *The Life of Herbert Hoover: Master of Emergencies, 1917–1918.* New York: W.W. Norton & Company, 1996.

Polikoff, Barbara G. *Herbert C. Hoover: Thirty-First President of the United States.* Ada, Okla.: Garrett Educational Corporation, 1990.

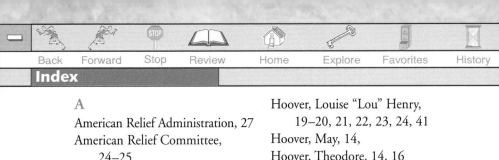

Index